COLOUR JETS

Colour Me Crazy

D1079389

Andrew Donkin
and Jeff Cummins

Collins

COLOUR JETS

For Graham Brand

First published in Great Britain
by HarperCollins*Publishers* Ltd 1996

The HarperCollins website address is
www.**fire**and**water**.com

12 11 10 9 8 7 6 5 4

Text © Andrew Donkin 1996
Illustrations © Jeff Cummins 1996

The author and illustrator assert the moral right to be
identified as the author and illustrator of the work.

A CIP record for this title is available
from the British Library.

ISBN 0 00 675154 7

Printed in Hong Kong

Chapter 1

Kevin was bored.

Walking home from school, he was big yawn, drop asleep, mind-numbingly bored. Every day Kevin followed the same route at the same time through the same dull streets.

Kevin couldn't understand why his housing estate hadn't been recognised as the most boring place in the whole world.

As far as Kevin was concerned, everything was dull. The buildings. The pavements. The walls. EVERYTHING!

BOREDOM CENTRAL

We could give you a tour but you wouldn't enjoy it

The only colour in the whole place came from the sun setting over the local waste tip. And that wasn't exactly a picture postcard.

As he walked on, Kevin smiled to himself, secretly. He was thinking about what he'd do later. Once it became dark, he'd be happy. Then he could get down to his real interest…

astronomy!

Kevin's thoughts were soon lost in deep space. He was thinking about all the brilliant discoveries he'd make.

He didn't look up.

He didn't look around him.

He didn't see the object that whizzed across the sky above him.

He was too busy looking forward to being sent to bed.

Chapter 2

When Kevin got home, things didn't get any brighter. Annoyingly, Kevin's parents even let him stay up late.

Until finally…

Kevin headed straight for his bedroom.

Inside, he threw open the window and got to work. Tonight's telescope target was the planet Jupiter.

Kevin's attic bedroom was perfect for astronomy. For a start, it was at least 7 metres nearer to Outer Space than the rest of the house.

Pretty soon, Kevin had finished his first observations and was relaxing.

That was when he saw it.

There was a weird light shooting across the night sky. Kevin watched it as it seemed to zigzag across the rooftops.

He quickly focused his telescope and realised what it was.

Luckily he stayed totally calm…

It's a U.F.O

…for about a tenth of a second!

I'VE SPOTTED A U.F.O!

Kevin grabbed his big torch. He pointed
it out of the window and began
to signal frantically. (He had
no idea what he was
signalling, but he
carried on
anyway.)

Suddenly the lights in the sky changed
course and headed straight for him!
Kevin swallowed hard.

Chapter 3

The lights swooped
down and flew towards
Kevin's house at an
incredible speed.

They got nearer!

AND NEARER!

13

The U.F.O. flew in through the window.
It illuminated Kevin's bedroom like a
giant floodlight.

He was totally
awe-struck!

Kevin quickly collected his thoughts.
This was a most excellent historical
happening.

Then he expressed greetings
on behalf of all
the people of
the Earth.

Err...

NASA

Hi Dudes!

As soon as he spoke, the circle of white lights split into seven smaller balls of energy. Each one was a different colour.

The lights flickered and gradually transformed into the solid body shapes of...

...Seven alien life forms!

The Spec-trums explained that they were alien day trippers. They were on Earth for a 24 hour visit.

Chapter 4

Kevin invited his alien guests to sit down. However, as the red Spec-trum sat down on Kevin's bed it turned bright red!

That's been happening since we arrived. Everything we touch changes colour!

Wow!

The blue Spec-trum thought it must be something to do with the Earth's climate.

Kevin wanted to see more.

So you could change this to green?

The green Spec-trum took Kevin's alarm clock and suddenly…

Brilliant!

Kevin soon had the aliens zapping every single thing in his bedroom.

How about a purple lampshade,

and a blue window,

and some yellow stripes on the wall,

and a green radiator,

Unfortunately, all the zapping was rather noisy and disturbed…

KEVIN!

Gulp! My dad! Quick, you'd better leave.

Nice meeting you, Kev. Bye!

Go and colour some other stuff.

The Spec-trums took flight.

Kevin was in trouble. If Dad saw his newly coloured bedroom, he'd go mad! Kevin turned out the light and dived into bed, pretending to be asleep.

Kevin? Are you flying that radio-controlled plane in here again? Kevin??

Luckily, Dad was fooled and soon went back to the television. Kevin curled up comfortably. What a night!

Chapter 5

Next morning, Kevin was in for a surprise at breakfast.

His dad was bright purple.

Kevin tried hard not to snigger.

Kevin left for school. Every day he followed the same route at the same time through the same dull streets.

Dull streets??

Kevin realised he had just walked past a purple and yellow spotted post box!

Those vandals have gone too far this time!

He looked around.
The houses on the estate
were every colour you
could imagine.

It seemed other people had noticed
too. They were standing around with
open mouths and bulging eyes.

25

Kevin walked over the purple and blue zebra crossing.

The world had gone colour crazy.

Chapter 6

Kevin went to Greenford School. When he arrived that morning, he found it wasn't just its name that was green!

Kevin thought it was brilliant!

Inside, everybody had plenty to talk about.

Only Kevin knew the truth
and he was keeping it to himself.

They all did their best, but it's hard to concentrate when your teacher is...

Right. Quiet please.

...blue with pink spots.

Everything kept going wrong – all day.

The headteacher, who liked things to be nice and neat and orderly, was having a hard time.

Science
Chemicals the wrong colour CANCELLED

Music
Piano keys all white   CANCELLED

Maths
Blackboards all purple   CANCELLED

Geography
Study maps all orange   CANCELLED

History
Teacher blue with pink spots CANCELLED

Art
Don't even ask!   CANCELLED!!

Finally she gave up.

In the middle of the afternoon, she sent the whole school home.

Chapter 7

Kevin walked part of the way home
with his friend, David. The streets were
strange and bizarre.

He thought about telling David his
secret, but he couldn't quite make up
his mind.

The two friends passed Mr Mason's carpet shop. There hadn't been a customer all day. His entire stock had gone one colour.

ANY COLOUR YOU WANT

AS LONG AS IT'S BLUE

Mr Mason had the blues in a big way.

Kevin began to feel a little uncomfortable.

They stopped at the traffic lights and waited.

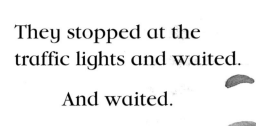

And waited.

And waited.

What's wrong?

After a few more minutes, Kevin realised what was happening. All the signal colours were wrong so no one was moving.

Just then the traffic lights changed from blue to orange. There hadn't been a green light for ages so Kevin decided to go for it.

Unfortunately, so did fifteen cars, three buses and two bicycles.

The result was a
right multi-coloured mess.

The drivers got out of their cars and started arguing about whose fault it was. They soon decided it was Kevin's.

Finally, a lady
at the back
spoke up.

It's not the boy's fault. The person to blame is whoever's responsible for all these colour changes.

Kevin and David sneaked away.

"Somebody's going to be for it when they get caught," said David.

Kevin could only smile weakly and agree. Maybe things weren't so brilliant.

Chapter 8

That evening, supper was a tense affair.

Afterwards, Mum suggested they all watch television. Their favourite programme was on at eight o'clock. She thought it would take their minds off things.

Now it's eight o'clock and time for... ... another special programme about the world colour crisis.

As they watched, Kevin sank lower and lower into his chair. If he'd sunk any lower, he'd have been in the cellar.

The President of the United States made a speech from the Orange House in Washington. The Russian leader made a public address from Blue-with-just-a-hint-of-green Square in Moscow. They both agreed that...

It's a disaster!

Kevin crept off to his bedroom.

The world was in chaos and it was all Kevin's fault.

Chapter 9

Knowing that he'd ruined the whole
world was a bit of a downer.
Kevin wanted to put it right.

He had to find the Spec-trums and see
if they could change things back to
normal.

Then Kevin caught sight of his green alarm clock. He suddenly remembered that the Spec-trums were only on Earth for a 24 hour visit!

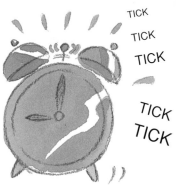

TICK
TICK
TICK
TICK
TICK

He realised he only had one hour to find them before they left the Earth for good.

And worse! The Spec-trums could be anywhere on the entire planet!

It was dark by now. Kevin quickly grabbed his telescope and threw open his bedroom window.

He started to scan all around the sky, looking for the aliens, straining his eyes for any lights that could be them.

43

All Kevin could see were the strange colours of the surrounding estate. Some of the buildings even glowed in the dark.

TICK
TICK

TICK
TICK

The aliens, however, were nowhere to be seen, and time was ticking away.

TICK

TICK

Chapter 10

Kevin took one last look. The whole landscape was a mixture of bizarre colours.

Everywhere – apart from one area of pure white light in the middle of the waste tip.

TICK

TICK

Defeated, Kevin flopped on his bed.

He intended to lie there and be very depressed for the rest of the night. He was just working his way up to being slightly depressed, when suddenly…

…inspiration struck!

Hadn't the Spec-trums been a white light the first time that he'd seen them flying over the rooftops? Kevin replayed the moment in his mind.

And, indeed, I think a replay will show that they were white. Very much so, in fact.

Kevin knew he had to check out the
waste tip. He put on his thick coat and
sneaked out.

Then
he ran
through
the multi-coloured
night, racing against time.

Now that he was outside and
alone, it suddenly all looked
rather spooky. There were
shadows everywhere.

Kevin ran as fast as he could.
He was worried that the white lights
might disappear before he could get there.

When Kevin reached the waste tip he
found the front gates firmly locked.
They were much too high to climb over.

Instead, he headed round
the side where he knew there was
a hole in the fence, and slipped through.

Inside, Kevin wove his way between the mountains of rubbish. He headed towards the source of the white light.

He kept going until…

It was the alien life forms, but not as he'd known them.

Chapter 11

The seven little aliens lay on the ground looking exhausted. What was worse, they were now all pale grey in colour.

I don't think the Earth's climate agrees with us.

We're all feeling rather ill.

The aliens really did look quite sick.
Nobody would have guessed that they'd
once been all the colours of the
rainbow.

I think you've overdone it, colouring the whole planet!

Kevin carefully picked up
one of the Spec-trums and
carried him out of the waste tip.

Kevin leaned the alien against a lamp post. As he did, a little of the green colour of the lamp post drained back into the Spec-trum. It gave Kevin an idea.

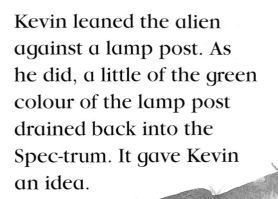

Could you absorb the colours? You know, take them back?

I don't know. I can try.

The Spec-trum concentrated hard. Then even harder. Finally, the colour began to slowly seep out of the lamp post and back into…

the Spec-trum!

A few minutes later he was back to normal.

"Now I'll go and absorb the green from everywhere else," said the Spec-trum happily.

Chapter 12

Kevin dashed back inside the waste tip. The other exhausted Spec-trums were still lying helplessly on the ground. Now he had to find a colour for each of them to absorb.

Some were easy.

And some were not.

Kevin had to run all over the estate
to find the colours he needed...

...and here's how he did it.

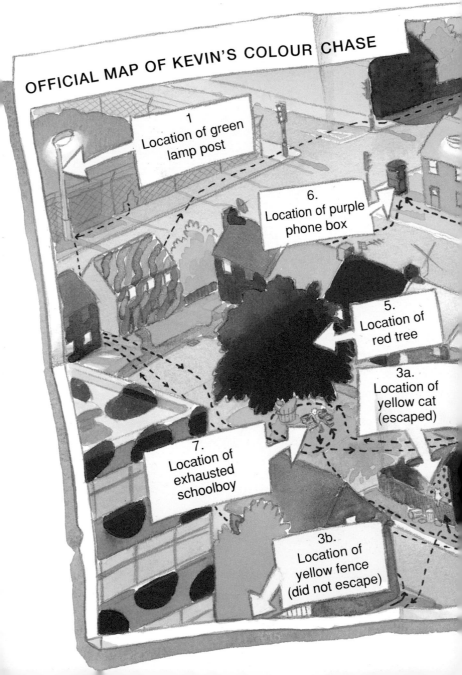

OFFICIAL MAP OF KEVIN'S COLOUR CHASE

1
Location of green lamp post

6.
Location of purple phone box

5.
Location of red tree

3a.
Location of yellow cat (escaped)

7.
Location of exhausted schoolboy

3b.
Location of yellow fence (did not escape)

Finally all the Spec-trums were re-coloured. All except for one.

Kevin hunted high and low for some orange, but he couldn't find the colour anywhere. The other Spec-trums were off putting the world to rights, but the one in Kevin's arms was fading fast.

> I do remember colouring the Great Wall of China. Could we go there?

Then he saw it.
The last bus of the evening.

The last **orange** bus of the evening.

Kevin gave chase.

At last the driver spotted Kevin.
He stopped the bus.

Wheeze!

L 10

The alien absorbed the orange.

Kevin absorbed the oxygen.

The bus driver was delighted to have his
bus back to its proper colour. In fact, he
was so happy he gave
Kevin and the
Spec-trum a
free ride
home.

That's just
the ticket,
that is.

Kevin waved goodbye to the orange Spec-trum as he flew off to meet his friends.

As soon as the Earth's colours were back to normal, they would return to their home planet.

Epilogue

When Kevin woke up the next morning, the first thing he did was reach for his alarm clock.

It wasn't green any more – just plain old grey.

Dad seemed back to normal as well...

Are you going to be in there all day, or what?

...unfortunately.

Outside, the world was grey in all the right places.

And it didn't seem boring at all.

Well, not that boring.